The Shropshire Parables

C C Mars

First Published 2025 by Idiolect
cover design Silke Mansholt
© C C Mars 2025

ISBN-13 -978-1-0683405-2-9
ISBN-10 -1-0683405-2-5

'That doesn't prove anything. After all, we've never had anyone from Bavaria staying till recently; damn those blue hills, I wish everyone would just forget about them.'

contents

Slightly Terminal

The pretty market town of Hearsay has a nearly brand-new MediCentre. On a fine autumn morning, Donna stands outside the clinic and looks at the names on the brass plaque by the door: Doctors Clamp, Poultice and Vile, as she has done so many times. They sound positively Dickensian; why couldn't it be Smith, Jones and Farmer? Especially that Doctor Vile – of course, nobody pronounces it like that; most say a sort of Frenchish *Veellay*. Donna has never heard the afflicted doctor saying his own name, not surprising really. Strange, she thinks, how words that mean nasty things sound nasty in themselves: vile, horrible, grotesque, say, compared to the floating niceness of words like beautiful or pretty with their dancing tongues on the back of your teeth.

1

'You going in or what?' A large lady startles Donna from her reverie. Donna stands aside and holds the door open for the woman who hobbles through.

'A thank you would have been nice,' Donna says to her back, but quietly; some of these biggies have a vicious right hook or at least a poison tip to their tongues. Donna follows her in; she is getting Clamp today who replaced the hapless Hu, who has now returned to Taiwan, undoubtedly fed up with the packs of children who followed him around singing *deedeelydee, deedeelydee, daa daa* and saying *exterminate* in their squeaky Dalek voices.

Bulky has taken her place at the counter and has got the bad cop of the two receptionists Donna is relieved to see. Donna years ago named the receptionists Sweet and Sour. She doesn't try to squeeze in but waves at the infinitely nicer Sweet over the shoulder of Big Bones.

'Donna Easton for Dr Clamp at ten-thirty.'

Sweet checks her computer,

'OK, please take a seat, Ms Easton.'

'Thanks,' Donna says thinking *nearly out of the woods.* But no, what's this, Large is finished checking in and goes to sit down? Receptionist Sour, now free, leans over and picks a little Post-it note from the front of Sweet's computer,

'Wait a moment Ms Easton; are you the girl with two phones?'

Donna blanches. She had indeed used two phones to get her appointment that morning, speaker phone in her lap and her mobile at her ear, both on speed dial with her trying to get through the impassable clump of calls from 8.00 am on, punching the redial buttons as soon as she got the engaged signal like some demented *Ninja*, all those wasted *PlayStation* years now paying off. After maybe fifty attempts she managed miraculously to get through at the same time to both Sweet and Sour at once and had surrealistically simultaneously booked two separate appointments for the same doctor. In a panic, she had reviewed her options – throw both phones into the sink: leave the country: never go back to the doctor ever again: start babbling incoherently. The last had won but how the confusion had sorted itself out has luckily left her with a three-minute post-traumatic amnesia situation.

She nods guiltily.

Sour symbolically tears the Post-it in two and tells her,

'It's very irresponsible behaviour; some of our patients calling in are seriously ill you know.'

Donna wonders to herself what seriously ill actually looks like – for all this woman knows Donna herself might be slightly terminal. She sucks in her cheeks and coughs before answering,

'Sorry about that; won't do it again.'

Sour dismisses her by picking up her coffee mug and turning to chat to Sweet.

Donna says softly to herself,

'*Be still my beating heart*,' and then turns to look around the waiting room for a possible seat.

The obvious choice is the middle one of three empty chairs near the door. But that is giving a hostage to fortune, putting yourself into the lap of the gods and also throwing caution to the winds. Who knows what randoms might enter in the next five minutes? You could easily be suddenly surrounded by some sneezing and coughing swine flu victim on one side and on the other a mother with mewling and puking child in arms, snot running down its face while it reaches out to pull your shiny earrings from the side of your head with its grubby little paws. Better the devil you know.

Donna turns on her emergency *Terminator Medical Diagnosis Scanner* to quickly check the current occupants. Three old ladies to the left, but no seats there anyway. Free seat in the middle of the other four by the window. Mrs. is on the right side with one shoe off and a pained expression. The *TMDS* goes into action and a little green dotted line traces her outline and a green typewriter text *DIAGNOSIS: BUNION* flashes up. Donna feels a wave of remorse about how she has been thinking about the poor woman. *Don't judge, she's probably a lovely person. I have to do better, and please, no more unpleasant derogatory names.* Anyway, getting back to the chair question, it is looking good so far on the right. On the other side, a chavvy fifteen-year-old couple, probably from the nearby Elton estate? She, with blonde hair scraped tightly back and he, with sleeveless tee-shirt the better to show off his three lions tattoo, the two of them chewing vigorously. *DIAGNOSIS: PREGNANCY CONFIRMATION* pops up.

Excellent, bunion and pregnancy, both non-airborne conditions as far as she knows. As Donna moves towards the seat the girl pops a loud, smacking bubble with evident relish, thick red lipstick and pink bubblegum remnants forming an unholy alliance around her mouth. Her boyfriend chuckles admiringly as the girl's tongue suggestively retrieves the lipstick/gum mixture for his benefit.

Donna has read that seventy-five per cent of lipstick is ingested by the woman wearing it; what happens to the other twenty-five per cent she wonders? Some on a tissue wiped off at night; some kissed away (although that sadly requires a current boyfriend); some smeared on the side of the faces of reluctant children kissed by aged aunts and some made into kiss marks on the back of love letters (once again boyfriend required).

The boy snorts and congratulates his girlfriend with a, 'Nice one.'

Definitely from the Elton estate. Donna jumps forward several years to imagine the two of them screaming at a little crew-cut-headed Tyson who has just dropped his ice cream outside the McDonald's on Hillstreet on a Wednesday morning.

'Now, now,' she says to herself for the second time today, 'there you go again, first the large lady and now this pair, don't be so *judgmental*. We are all God's children.'

Although now she thinks of it, some Americans seem to think we might all be that Spaghetti Monster's children. She imagines going to the church of the Spaghetti Monster and taking communion there with perhaps a small bowl of linguine representing the body of the Son of SM and a small trickle of arrabbiata sauce as His blood (or maybe Her blood? Hard to tell as we are obviously not made in the Spaghetti Monster's image, at least not all of us). Also didn't some Dutch woman get permission to wear a colander instead of a helmet (as it was deemed religious headwear) when riding her scooter - a Pastafarian practice that has not reached Hearsay so far?

Donna eases into the vacant seat and sighs loudly; she hates having her ears waxed or is it de-waxed or maybe un-waxed - no, no, it's irrigated, isn't it, like a field? However much you are expecting it a flood of warm liquid into your ear always comes as something of a shock. And then you have to do it again on the other side. And afterwards on the way home - walking along with *Vulcan* hearing, a bit like Jack Nicholson in that *Wolf* film after he gets bitten - she will be able to hear an insect sneezing in a tree from two miles away - a recalcitrant trickle of water running coldly down her neck.

'Should have brought a book, should have brought a book, should have brought a book,' she hums to herself. She looks down at the pile of *Hello* magazines on the little table. *Terminator Germ Scanner* on - the magazines turn bright yellow with green smudges, the residues of hundreds of sweaty nervous hands. Eeugh. Hey, didn't she touch the door handle on the way in? She puts her offending right hand firmly in her pocket; that will stay there till we get to some soapy hot water – we don't want those difficult little clostridiums running amok everywhere after all.

'Should have brought a book, should have brought a book.' She looks up at the posters. Oh! A new one, joy unbounded!

Pneumococcal vaccination: were you around in 1941?

No other information, just a little email address at the bottom to reply to. 1941? Maybe there was something wrong with the vaccine? Still, they have left it a bit late if that was the case, *yeh, I was wondering why I've been feeling a little unwell for the last sixty-eight years?*

Donna turns her attention to the clouds outside. Now are they cirrus, or cumulus; surely she just saw this on the telly the other day? In one ear and out the other she thinks ironically, or is it tragically?

'Ms Easton,' Sour calls out to her, 'can you go through?'

Ms Easton does not move.

DrainMeisters

Andy and Samo barrel into the pretty market town of Hearsay in their white van complete with huge DrainMeister signs on both sides.

'Thirty-seven minutes from Wolverhampton, that's what I call motoring,' Andy declares in triumph.

They do a two-wheeler, cornering into Moorstreet; it is an emergency after all.

Samo has been going,

'Na-na, na-na,' out the window, 'in *loo* of a siren,' as he says.

They pull up at number seventeen where an anxious Mrs Thankman is waiting for them in the doorway; she waves. Andy sighs, she is obviously over their thirty-five-year cut-off point. He fondly remembers the time the two of them

7

turned up to rescue three twenty-year-old girl students from an overflowing toilet. The mathematically challenged Samo had thought two into three doesn't go but after a bit of fiddling around two into three had gone, and with none left over. Happy days.

As they saunter up the drive Andy shouts,

'Mrs Thankman, you got anywhere for me to charge my mobile, battery's going?'

She looks at the pair of them, also with disappointment; both have spiky gelled hair, Andy has a little diamante thing hanging from his left ear, Samo has a pierced eyebrow – she doesn't have a cut-off age but is not hopeful of any action from these two who could be headed for a disco.

She shows Andy a socket in the hall and he plugs his phone in saying,

'You, are a diamond geezer. Take us to your loo, dear.' Samo laughs though he has heard that one many times.

She shows them to a pristine downstairs toilet.

Andy peers into the bowl,

'So this is where the little bleeder went down?'

She nods.

'And you haven't used it since?'

'No of course not; we've been using the upstairs one since the erm - incident.'

'Better get on the big glove then; any chance of a coffee?'

Mrs Thankman nods and bustles off to her kitchen.

Andy puts on a massive pink rubber glove that goes all the way up to his shoulder. He kneels down and thrusts his hand into the toilet and round the bend,

'Reminds me of last night with Franki,' he says to Samo.

'She your new girlfriend then?'

'Yep.'

'Isn't she a bit of a tart, that Franki?'

Andy freezes with his hand still round the bend.

'You what?' he says menacingly.

Samo steps back slightly before Andy relaxes and grins toothily,

'Yep, she is a bit. Here, give us your pencil, Samo.'

Andy uses the pencil to get a little extra reach round the U-bend.

'Nope, nothing here, not - a - sausage,' he laughs but Samo doesn't get it, maybe next time, or maybe the time after?

Andy hands the pencil back to Samo who looks at it suspiciously before putting it back in his top pocket.

Andy stands up his arm dripping.

'Hey, you look like a giant lobster,' Samo says.

Andy stretches out the pink lobster arm clicking his thumb and fingers together towards Samo's face whispering,

'Beware the LobsterMen.'

'Watch it, you don't know where that thing's been,' Samo protests.

Mrs Thankman comes into the crowded toilet with two mugs of coffee and some Kit Kats.

'Magic,' says Samo. 'My favourites.'

Andy takes a big swig from the mug and says,

'Looks like a job for Cyclops, Samo, c'mon.'

They go out to their van and lug a huge television with miles of umbilical cable up the drive; on the way Andy starts singing,

My baby has gone down the plughole
My baby has gone down the plug,

Samo joins in halfway through,

'The poor little thing
Was so skinny and thin
She ought to have been barfed in a jug
She ought to have been barfed in a jug.'

In the last line they do a little harmony.

'We should be on *Britain's Got Talent,*' Samo tells Mrs Thankman who smiles politely.

They plug in the big television outside the loo and it springs to life.

'What is that?' Mrs Thankman asks.

'It's the all-seeing eye,' Andy tells her. 'Watch this.'

He switches on the light at the end of the tube and points it at her face,

'Look, you're on the telly, everybody gets their fifteen minutes, eh.'

Mrs Thankman looks at her garishly lit face on the screen; it seems hideously distorted as if she is looking through a fishbowl, she still adjusts her hair though.

'Same thing as that colonoscopy thing they have in hospitals except there they shove it up your...'

'Andy,' Samo cautions.

'Oops, nearly said a bad word. Anyway, we send a light where the sun don't shine. It's our motto.' He turns round and sure enough, the slogan is emblazoned on the back of his tee shirt with a little drawing of a sun with rays under the DrainMeisters inscription.

'How did it happen anyway?' Samo asks Mrs Thankman as they gulp their coffee.

'My grandson Tyger, he's only three, he thought the dog was dirty and put him in the toilet bowl for a wash and pulled the flush.'

'Well, if it's any comfort it happens all the time,' says Andy reassuringly.

'And are they all OK?' Mrs Thankman asks.

'Course not, fish food usually, but if anyone can save him we are the ones.'

Andy takes another swig from the mug and then balances it on the cistern before plunging the end of the cable down the loo and navigating it round the bend while Samo watches the monitor out in the hall. Andy provides a commentary in a breathy Attenboroughish voice as the camera snakes down.

'In the murky waters of the Amazon lurk strange creatures which…'

'Hey, go back a bit,' Samo interrupts, 'I thought I saw something move.'

Andy pulls back the camera into the filthy void above the water line.

'Look, where the vent pipe comes in,' Samo shouts, 'He's caught in the trap.'

Cue for Andy to break into song again,

'We're caught in a trap.

I can't walk out.

Because I love you too much ba-by.'

As Andy sings he curls up his top lip in best Elvis style.

Samo claps.

'Nice acoustics in this toilet,' says Andy.

'What did you mean by *trap*?' Mrs Thankman asks.

'It's the space where all the poopy bad smells get captured and then they go up the vent pipe to the top of the house where they can waft all over Hearsay,' Andy answers.

'See if you can angle the camera, Andy, get a better picture?' asks Samo.

Andy twists the cable a bit and sure enough you can see something cowering in the start of the vent pipe.

'He's scared shitless, poor little mite,' Samo says squatting down to look at the TV.

'Unfortunately not,' says Andy coming through and examining the picture more closely.

'How will you get him out?' asks Mrs Thankman.

'Let's take a look at the vent pipe,' Andy says and the three go out and round to the back of the house the boys still cradling their near-empty mugs.

They look at the vent pipe thoughtfully; Samo puts his hand around it,

'Pretty small?'

Andy stamps on the ground,

'Concrete, we could drill down; got a pneumatic in the van; little bugger might jump when he hears the noise.'

They think a bit more; Andy finally decides,

'Nah, toilet's going to have to come out.'

They go back in and after undoing some bolts heave out the toilet unceremoniously with an ominous creaking sound.

'I'll get some newspaper,' says Mrs Thankman; too late a trail of water from the bowl is already seeping into the corridor carpet.

Andy puts the big glove on again.

'Revenge of the LobsterMen, part two,' he declares and lies full length on the floor plunging his arm down the large hole in the ground they have just created.

'Shove the camera down the side, Samo, I haven't a clue where I am.'

Samo pushes the camera tube down the side of Andy's arm. He sits at the screen and starts directing him,

'Left a bit, up a bit, Bernie the Bolt, down a bit, yep, yep, nope, the little bugger has gone up the vent, you scared him.'

'What's his name?' Andy asks Mrs Thankman.

'Goliath,' she answers.

'Goliath?'

'It was ironic.'

'Here, I've got an idea, give me a bit of that Kit Kat,' Andy tells Samo.

'I thought that chocolate was bad for dogs?' Mrs Thankman asks.

'If that is the case, then he's had it. He's covered in the stuff,' Andy says crudely.

He plunges back down into the hole with a bit of the bar saying,

'Here, Kitty, Kitty.'

'I thought it was a dog?' Samo asks.

'A dog that speaks English?' Andy replies, 'Anyway I was talking about the biscuit, dufus.'

'He's coming, he's coming,' says Samo.

Nobody breathes and then suddenly Andy jerks,

'Got him, that was close. Pull the camera up first, Samo, might be a tight squeeze.'

Samo pulls up the tube and then Andy slowly brings his arm out holding a pathetic little ball of matted fur, unrecognisable as anything alive.

'What kind is he?' he asks Mrs Thankman.

'Pekinese.'

'Pekinese? Well he certainly comes from the Ming dynasty now,' says Andy holding his nose with his free hand, 'here you better take him.'

Mrs Thankman picks up a towel and takes the mutt.

Andy starts taking off the big glove saying,

'Your little Tyger was right though; he does need a bath, but please Mrs Thankman...'

'Yes?'

'Keep the plug in this time.'

Fire Pig

Some say that the centre of the pretty market town of Hearsay is Ramamurthi's Convenience Store and that you can buy absolutely anything there. Indeed, on the shop counter is a little statue like those three wise monkeys but these three are called Nosee, Askee and Getsee. Basically, you tell them (the Ramamurthis not the monkeys) what they *don't have* and next day they *do have*. Simples. Just between us, a bit of an urban myth has grown up among the youth of Hearsay that if you touch the head of little Getsee three times then that very evening you will be more likely to *get some* if you know what I mean - well that would explain why Getsee's head is a little shinier than his friends.

At 6.55 a.m. sharp Mrs Ramamurthi (Sheela to her friends) as always shoos away the crows from the filled-to-bursting black bin liners in front of the shop. She addresses them sternly,

'Next month the parish is introducing big metal bins and it will be the end of your free lunches from the black bin bags. You will tell your grandchildren of this golden age, this time of plenty, these halcyon days and they will not believe you.'

She wags her index finger at them to emphasise the point.

The crows wait patiently till she goes inside, they are wise enough to live in the moment and will *Carpe the old Diem* out of the current bags and let tomorrow look after itself.

Sheela undoes the massive padlocks and pulls up the heavy metal blinds. As always, she curses the garish fake graffiti on them. The rep had told her it was perfect to deter the real graffiti boys but then what was the point? The locals would have done it for free while on the other hand she'd had to pay for this nonsense. Also, to be honest, the pretty market town of Hearsay is not really known for its rampant youth culture. Plus, any local graffitists (if that is the word?) would have bought their spray cans from the Ramamurthi shop at a considerable markup, unlike the geezers brought down from Wolverhampton who had supplied their own paint and insisted on tea and free Snickers from the store.

Sheela goes into the shop, flicks on the fluorescents and after a quick check to see no one is coming pulls up the loose board next to the till and fishes out her new book, still in its film covering, no time yesterday to even peek inside. She bangs the kettle on and runs her nail down the book's plastic wrapper which crinkles up into a tiny white wrinkly ball.

'So, entropy, who can stop your relentless progress?' she sighs and tosses the ball to the bin, it balances on the rim, wobbles a bit, and then falls outside. She sighs again before popping a teabag into her mug, filling it up and then turning back to her new book *World Horoscopes, Know Yourself (Volume 4 Chinese Zodiac)*. She checks the door again, it wouldn't do for Mr Ramamurthi (Vikram to his friends) to find out about this, he doesn't approve of such books. She had left him in the land of nod twenty minutes before and is not really worried he will turn up, sleeping (along with eating) is one of his special powers.

She keeps her fingers crossed that this new *Volume 4* will be more positive than *Volume 3 (Heliocentric Astrology)* which was very disappointing. She leafs through to the back pages where the birth dates are indexed – she is 1st July 1947. What will she be? Hmm, slap bang in the middle of the Fire Pigs. That doesn't sound too good. Better check out the *Famous Pigs* first of all. Here we are… Henry Kissinger. There is a little picture of his face grinning away. Mrs Ramamurthi sighs. Who else? Chiang Kai-shek. Another grinning warmonger no doubt. She turns the page. Oh dear, Julie Andrews. Not very good company at all. Hang on, wait a moment, these are just pigs in general, in fact, Julie Andrews is a Wood Pig and Henry Kissinger is a Water Pig. Phew. But good old Chiang Kai is definitely Fire Pig, nevertheless some improvement anyway.

She does some calculations; twelve animal signs and five whatever-they-ares means that there is a Firepig year every sixty years. So, logically, one in sixty people is a Firepig, now, how many people come into the shop every day? A couple of hundred regulars and a few dozen randoms so that means at least three of their customers are Firepigs, but who? They would have to be around seventy-two years old, or possibly twelve, one hundred and thirty-two seems unlikely though some customers do look like it...

Just then she hears the sound of Laurie's scooter pulling up outside, no missing that hideous rasping. She looks out the window and sees Laurie grab a bundle of *Hearsay Star and Gazettes* from his little trailer. He heaves them in the shop door saying,

'Morning Mrs R.,' pops the papers on their stand and gets his Stanley knife out to cut the plastic ties.

'Laurie?'

'Yep,'

'What's your date of birth and year?'

'Twenty-third Feb. nineteen ninety-one, why?'

'Just got a new Chinese Astrology book, wait a mo.'

Sheela flicks to the back again and tells him,

'You're a Metal Sheep.'

'Come again?'

'It's your Chinese sign. You are a Metal Sheep.'

'That good?'

'Let's see, famous Metal Sheep, oh, Gorbachev?'

'That Russian geezer?'

'Yep, with the mark on his head. Look, here is his picture. And Rupert Murdoch?'

Laurie looks blank

'The newspaper guy, ironically,' Sheela points down at the bundle he has just opened. She carries on looking,

'Ah, maybe you know this one, Leonard Nimoy?'

'Oh yeh, Mr Spock. That's cool. Can't stay to chat though, busy, busy, busy, live long and prosper.'

After he's gone Mrs Ramamurthi says to herself,

'Well, I think you did better than me there, Laurie.' She decides to abandon the *Famous Pigs* and turns to the *Fire Pigs - Hugs and Cuddles* section. Let's see, this should be interesting. She reads carefully out loud,

'It's true that Fire Pigs have to work pretty hard to get something in return, but oh my, don't they receive big dividends? Lucky in love. Lucky in life.' She nods. Could be worse. Could be worse.

The little shop doorbell tinkles and Mrs Ramamurthi quickly slips the book under the till, but on looking up it's not Vikram but only Unwashed George come for his daily supplies. Mrs Ramamurthi heaves his two bottles of White Lightning onto the counter. As always, she imagines that the lightning tangles on the label signify the type of hangover you are going to get from the contents but she knows Unwashed George has the perfect hangover remedy, i.e. more of the same, those bottles contain both cause and cure in cider form. Unwashed counts out his pennies carefully onto the counter and Mrs R scoops them onto a magazine and then into the till with her sleeve, trying not to touch them too much.

'George,' (she never uses his first name), 'would you say I am *lucky in love?*'

George looks her up and down thoughtfully.

Then thinks for a bit.

Finally, he answers,

'I'd give you one.'

'Get out of my shop this minute, you bad man!' Mrs Ramamurthi shouts banging her book on the counter for extra effect.

George grabs his bottles and exits speedily murmuring softly,

'You did ask.'

Once he is gone Mrs Ramamurthi sits down again and gets out her little mirror.

'Sheela, you've still got it,' she smiles, wagging the self-same finger at herself this time.

Not a Story

In the more upmarket side of the pretty market town of Hearsay, Edie maintains a tidy house. Today she is giving the downstairs windows a once over with her new German *Window Vac* which makes such short work of them that she wishes she had more panes to clean. She wonders about offering the neighbours a once over for their windows but decides they might think she was casting aspersions on their cleanliness. She imagines if old Tom Sawyer had had one of these devices and enough windows he could have retired. As she is emptying the dirty water tank of the *Window Vac* she hears a faint noise at the door. When she opens, she is surprised to see a dark brown cat sitting on her natural coir doormat.

'*The cat sat on the mat is not a story. The cat sat on the other cat's mat is a story,*' she says to the cat. The cat looks curiously past her.

'I guess you are not familiar with the work of the great John le Carré?'

The cat seems to be sniffing the air, perhaps checking for dog smells?

'If I had a cat then that might be the other cat's mat but as I don't then it's not and therefore it's not a story, is it?'

Still no response.

'What's your name anyway?'

Yet again no answer. The cat saunters past her and bounds up the stairs. A few minutes later Edie hears a bumping noise from her bedroom. She hurries up and at first she can't see where the little one has gone, but after a moment realises he has jumped with the help of some old boxes onto the top of her wardrobe and settled down on a folded pink blanket up there.

'Make yourself at home, why don't you?'

The cat does a three-sixty-degree turn and settles down exactly where he was without even opening his eyes.

Edie leaves him to it.

For lunch Edie prepares herself some nice sandwiches with some fresh Parma ham from Astrid's Deli. A little expensive for a cat but she relents and puts a few slices on a saucer and takes it up to the bedroom.

'Look what I've got for you?'

She wafts the saucer around to tempt him with the aroma but the cat doesn't bat an eyelid.

She puts the saucer down next to the wardrobe saying,

'Suit yourself, see if I care.'

At ten to six Edie hears a scratching sound at the door. Sitting at the bottom of the stairs is the cat looking impassive.

'Your lordship deigns us with his regal presence?'

Nothing.

Edie opens the door and the cat saunters out into the night.

She calls after it,

'Thank you for coming. Arrivederci amore.'

Next morning Edie's attention is focused on some specks of black mould in the downstairs loo. They are microscopic but she has got some powerful anti-fungal grout treatment from Ramamurthi's Store anyway. However, before she even has her rubber gloves on, she hears the front door.

There he is, this time without hesitating for any chitchat he is up the stairs and hearing the same banging from yesterday Edie decides not to follow him up and gets back to her mould. At lunchtime she puts a sardine on a saucer (although the ham from yesterday had been untouched) and takes it up with a little bowl of water.

'Room service,' she calls out as she enters the bedroom, no response.

Day three same again but this time Edie doesn't bother to supply lunch. Well, he has turned his nose up both times and today she is not going to give him the opportunity of a third strike,

'If you are hungry you can come to the kitchen like a proper waif and stray,' she shouts after him as he goes up the stairs.

Day four she blocks the cat's entry.

'We need a name if you are going to continue calling.'

The cat moves side to side but Edie tracks his movements to stop him passing. She had been thinking at first of calling him Karla to keep the Le Carré connection but now she sees him again she's not sure he really is a Karla. She had been disappointed with the new Oldman film, she has a fondness for the old Alec Guinness version, but now her mind is made up,

'I have decided to name you Smiley for obvious reasons.' On that, she lets Smiley past, up the stairs and then hears him clumping up onto the wardrobe.

Smiley comes every weekday but on Saturdays and Sundays has the day off. On the ninth day, Edie decides to follow him when he leaves in the evening. The night before she had watched *the French Connection* and knows that you really should have two or ideally three cops for perfect surveillance, preferably in radio contact and keeping one in front of the suspect. However, needs must and as it is only her it will have to be a bit more of a shifty *Miss Marple* affair. After Smiley leaves, she quickly pops on a baseball cap and dark glasses and slips out into the evening after him. Smiley marches up Brook Ave and while keeping a good speed doesn't look round and seems to have no interest in whether anyone is following him. Edie sticks to the shadows just in case.

Halfway up Moorstreet, tragedy, Celia and Tobias are out pruning their azaleas. Edie thinks of turning back home but too late, they have spotted her and wave. Edie is suddenly conscious of her dark glasses and baseball cap.

Celia speaks first,

'Out for an evening stroll?' Is there a note of suspicion in her voice?

'Yes, just catching a bit of fresh air before dinner. Azaleas are looking good.' In actual fact, she thinks the plants look a little sad, and would be better off in a more sheltered spot.

In the distance, from the corner of her eye, she can just make out Smiley turning into Hazel Ave. She will lose him if she is not careful and she can't risk following him again if he always comes up this way as she imagines these two are always tinkering around in their garden.

'Must dash,' she says and hurries up the street.

Tobias waves his shears at her,

'Don't you live that way?'

'Shortcut,' is all she can come up with.

At Hazel Ave she thinks she has lost track but just spots Smiley's tail as he turns into the new builds down the end. She speed walks up to the turning and sees him entering the last house of the row. She now walks casually up to case the joint. Fairly new car in the drive. Nothing to see really. So, this is Smiley Mansions? Hmm.

For nine months Smiley continues to turn up every weekday apart from at Christmas and New Year. He has developed a gentle knocking technique. One time Edie tells him,

'We have a bell you know but I guess you probably prefer old school.'

In all his visits Smiley never touches any food or drinks any water. One time Edie bends down at the door to stroke him but Smiley pulls away from her hand with not exactly a growl but some muttering of disapproval. Edie straightens up saying,

'Ok, ne me touché pas, I get it. Fair enough.'

Then, on Shrove Tuesday, Smiley doesn't show. She looks out the door half a dozen times just in case but no sign. That evening she doesn't really enjoy her pancakes. Wednesday and Thursday also no show.

On Friday Edie decides to investigate. She follows his route carefully, looking under hedges and bushes, just in case, but thankfully no little body is lying there. At last, she gets to the newbuilds and carefully approaches his house. No car in the driveway, no curtains in the windows. She peeps in and the house is completely deserted, no furniture, nothing. In some ways it's good news, but...

On her way back home, Edie goes through the park and decides to sit on one of the benches. There are a couple of lads passing a ball to each other on the grass. She watches them for maybe ten minutes. She hopes little Smiley has found a new wardrobe with a new pink blanket on it. She starts crying softly.

The Green Man

To the north of the pretty market town of Hearsay is the tiny village of Nivver. We say village but apart from the old Methodist church and around thirty houses, there is only one shop which is nearly never (excuse the pun) open.

Nivver had its fifteen minutes of fame when it got its first, and only, traffic lights. That day I can tell you was a day of party. Some say the traffic upgrade happened because Hearsay's Chief of Police, Inspector Fine, was driving home along the north road back from Much Wenlock with his wife at around a hundred and ten in his new Audi. Just at that moment, Aled (who owns a small farm adjoining the village, maybe one-fifty acres growing mostly sprouts and peas) chose to drive his tractor round the corner of the Methodist church

- for its age it still has quite a turn of speed (the tractor that is). Inspector Fine had to swerve violently to avoid catastrophe and his wife got her hot coffee in her lap. Wheels, as they say, were set in motion that day, and six months later two old guys arrived from Birmingham and set up the new lights – *state of the art* - or so they said.

At the grand opening ceremony Revd. Wood from the church cuts the ribbon between the traffic lights with the biggest pair of scissors you have ever seen (he borrowed them from the haberdashery in Preen where they normally occupy the window display along with enormous needles and a giant cotton reel) and little Bertha, only seven years old, is the first to press the pedestrian crossing button. Bowman, the local chef de partie who works in Walsall at the *Maison de Joie*, has even made a cake with red, orange and green sections for the watching crowd. Everybody agrees that Nivver is finally on the map. Happy days.

Next morning at breakfast the good Pastor scans the *Hearsay Star and Gazette,* he has high hopes that the enormous scissors will have got him in (he made sure the reporter and photographer got extra-large slices of cake) at last but no, there is only a picture of the little grinning Bertha pressing the stupid crossing button. The Revd. folds the paper resignedly and tells Martika, his housekeeper,

'Never work with animals or children.'

Martika, who also does his accounts, the Revd. is a dunce with figures, refrains from pointing out that one-third of his income comes from baptisms, (the animals bit she agrees with having been once bitten by an Alsatian in Prague - the dog that is, not someone from Alsace).

However, other problems appear that very morning. The B4689 as you are probably aware, is not so busy these days. In fact, since the Audi incident, Aled has refused to drive his tractor on it – he claims he could see the look of horror on the faces of the Inspector and his good wife as they approached him at high speed and thought his final moment had come - though to be honest his tractor is built like a tank and the Audi would have definitely suffered more. Also, come to think of it, the Inspector seems to take a different route when he makes his weekly trip to Much Wenlock for his favourite pork sausages. This means as far as traffic goes (apart from Sundays when the faithful Methodists from Hearsay make their virtuous trek out to church) Doctor Clamp drives through at eight in the morning and back at six-thirty and that is it, give or take.

Unfortunately, Nivver local Birgitta lives on one side of the road just next to the crossing and her mother within spitting distance on the opposite side. They both moved from Ostfriesland in North Germany in 1966 (not a good year, but once again another story) and bought identical houses on either side of the road – *close but not too close* as they say. Like the rest of the village, Birgitta is very impressed with the new crossing and at precisely seven-thirty that morning as usual she sets off to make her mother's breakfast coffee, the old lady is getting on a bit. After inspecting the crossing handiwork, there does seem to be a little untidiness at the base, Birgitta presses the button and looks up at the little red man. Then she gazes up the road, it is almost straight and you can see all the way up to Aled's farmhouse a good fifteen-minute walk away. The heat makes the air shimmer a little over the empty tarmac. Good to have time to think, to clear the mind. She looks up at the church roof, notices a few loose tiles and makes a mental note to tell the Revd. about them next time she sees him. She presses the button again, a little more firmly this time, then twice more for good measure. She smooths down her blouse and notices a little thread of lint which she carefully removes. She studiously avoids looking at the little men, *a watched kettle never boils,* as they say. Suddenly the crossing starts peeping and she looks up to see the little green man, she nods politely to him and crosses.

Granny Wiebke is a little put out by Birgitta's tardiness and is already sitting at the breakfast table. She is even more put out when Birgitta tells her that in her excitement at using the new crossing, she has left the morning ham back in her house.

'I get it, it only take a moment,' she tells her mother. Fifteen minutes later she returns with the ham, Granny Wiebke is not happy.

On her seventh trip across the road, Birgitta decides to take the big clock from the mantelpiece to time the crossing – she doesn't have a watch. The clock is rather heavy, several kilos, and doesn't have a second hand but it is the best she has. She waits till it clicks the minute, presses the button, and then starts counting her pink elephants which she knows are roughly one second.

Six minutes and twenty elephants later the crossing is activated. On the way back it is just a few elephants short of seven minutes.

That afternoon Birgitta gets a pencil and a big sheet of paper, a glass of plum brandy and starts doing some calculations. Six minutes and forty seconds on average to change the lights and for the green man to appear. As she crosses the street at least twenty times a day to look in on her mother, that makes one hundred and thirty-three and one-thirds minutes every day or approximately seven hundred hours per year (the mother comes to stay with her for Christmas and Ascension, thank God). All in all, one month of her life gone to worshipping the little green idol every year.

After two painful months she tells her friend Max that she thinks she sees one of the little red men grinning at her and that he has little devil's horns too. Max gets out his wooden ladder and at great danger to life and limb climbs up to inspect. When he gets up closer, he discovers the grin and horns are just some random bird poop on the little red man's face and he wipes them off with his sleeve.

Birgitta soldiers on through the summer and even one afternoon when she is desperate for the loo she sneaks across the street with the red man showing. That night she can't sleep for worry about security cameras and the arrival of a burly sergeant from Hearsay. In the morning a loud knock on the door makes her jump from her bed, convinced she is going to be locked up, but it is only the post with a parcel for her neighbour.

The other villagers can see she is becoming worn out and so organise a collection to buy her a timer. Now six minutes before she wants to cross, she can go out and press the button, start her timer, and go back for her morning tea. Then, six minutes later when she walks out, she likes to snap her fingers at the little men just at the right time to keep them on their toes. Unfortunately, Birgitta is unable to think of nineteen other tasks apart from her morning tea she can perform in exactly six minutes.

A year and a half later two guys (I think it may have been the same ones that put up the crossing in the first place) are installing the Revd's fibre-optic broadband and as they are finishing up accidentally cut the power supply to the traffic lights. Some nasty-looking sparks are coming from the two cable ends so they quickly fill in the hole as it is late, jump in their truck and head back to Birmingham leaving the traffic lights dark and silent. The next morning the Revd. finds Birgitta praying in the church. As she stands up, she tells him,

'Revd., there IS a God.'

The good Revd. wipes his brow with his big white handkerchief and says,

'Birgitta, I can tell you with hand on heart, that knowledge is a great relief to me.'

Well, of course, things in Nivver have returned to normal these days, but Birgitta still sometimes presses the button before crossing the street. Her little friends of course don't appear, I think she misses them.

Roadwork Poets

The pretty market town of Hearsay's premier (actually its only these days) newspaper is the *Star and Gazette*, and its number one reporter is Maisi Dukes.

One evening she is driving back from a boring meeting about circulation in Wolverhampton when the road (the B4744) feels a little bumpy. A gleam of an idea for a new pothole article for next week's *Friday Special* issue causes her to pay particular attention to the road surface. As much as the citizens of Hearsay hate potholes they love even more hearing about how terrible they are.

Peering through the twilight at the road ahead Maisi crazily thinks she just made out an ampersand? Probably just bad light? She slows up a bit anyway and ten metres on she sees another? Maisi didn't win Shropshire's *Golden Pen Investigator Award* (she has the little statuette on her mantle piece) for nothing.

She stops her car and reverses cautiously, the winding B roads around Hearsay are notorious for their boy racers (we already encountered Inspector Fine and his new Audi, then there is Max with his Maserati, and... in fact, the cyclists of Hearsay are intimately acquainted with the hedges and bushes that border those B roads and can often be seen pulling twigs and leaves from their hair while cursing softly).

Sure enough, there is the ampersand on the road, strangely pixelated and in a slightly different colour of tarmac, but definitely an ampersand. Maisi gets out her mobile and takes a few pics. She drives on slowly and there on the road is a third. Further on she sees what appears to be a question mark? Curiouser and curiouser. After that all the way back to Hearsay, despite keeping a careful eye out, Maisi sees no more untoward marks. She wonders if maybe the markings were just natural patterns caused by some drainage structure or wiring or whatever?

Next morning in the *Star and Gazette* office Maisi asks if anyone has noticed anything about the roads around the town. Carlos the printer reminds her of the story she covered in Nivver regarding the new traffic lights there. Maisi shudders as she remembers the enormous piece of orange cake with an unpleasant aftertaste the Pastor had given her - he had even watched her eat it so it wasn't possible to dump it.

More interestingly the paper's sub-editor Jesus (he comes from Mexico but has now given up trying to persuade people to pronounce his name correctly as Hesus) says he noticed quite a bit of bumpiness on the B4830 coming in to work.

'Gracias Jesus,' Maisi tells him, 'I'm on my way.' Either she finds more ampersands or failing that some good material for her pothole story, win-win.

Once on the B4830 she does notice the road feels very slightly lumpy but can't make out anything in particular apart from a few circles. It is only on the way back that she comes across a series of three large Ys between the Os.

Back at the *Star and Gazette* office, she sets up a whiteboard (inspired by *Vera* the TV cop) and draws a little map with Hearsay at the centre and the two offending roads.

Under she puts,

B4744 & & & ?

B4830 Y O Y O Y

She calls in her make-do investigation team of Jesus and Carlos to assist.

Carlos comes up with the obvious *yo-yo* for the second road but why the extra Y?

Maisi muses on the possibility of *YO YO* as in yes yes? Maybe the third O was lost?

Jesus favours the more poetic interpretation of *'why oh why oh why'*.

Maisi likes Jesus's suggestion and adds,

'In that case maybe the first is something like *AND AND AND WHAT?*'

'Could be,' says Jesus, 'but why don't you just ask?'

'Ask who?' Maisi enquires.

'Whoever mended the road of course?'

'Which is whom?'

Jesus raises his hands to the heavens,

'You're the star journalist, Maisi, not me, I just correct your grammar.'

Maisi rolls her sleeves up and gets to work. First, she rings the Department of Road and Transport but they refuse to give out personal information on their workers or contractors. Hmm. Then the Parish Council, no luck there. Finally, kicking herself, she recalls her mentor's famous saying, *what is a journalist's favourite part of a horse? It's mouth of course.* Simples, where in Shropshire are there roadworks at present? There is a folder of all current works in the paper's archives. Yep, nearest is on the A5 between Shrewsbury and Oswestry. Maisi hops in her car and an hour later, when she reaches the spot, for the first time in her life, she is happy to see cones, traffic lights and diversion signs. Parking in a nearby lay by she approaches a group of geezers having a fag and a cup of tea.

'Hello, I'm from the *Hearsay Star and Gazette*,' she says showing her little card.

The leader of the workers sighs and says,

'Please, not more about potholes, you guys got nothing better to do than harass us, day in day out?'

Maisi holds her hand up,

'No, no, nothing about potholes. I was wondering if you did these road repairs on the B4744?' She shows him some of her pictures.

'No, no, that's too small for us, we don't do those little B roads, that'll be subcontracted out to one of the little independents. Any ideas?' he turns to his crew.

One of the older guys answers,

'Could be Tunde and his son, came over from Lagos about twenty years back, they do a ton of B stuff, always borrowing bits and pieces from us. Nice pair.'

Maisi asks him,

'Do you have an address?'

'Nope, but they live over in Market Downe. You'll find them easy, it's tiny.'

Market Downe is indeed tiny and the first person Maisi asks points out the house.

A woman answers the door,

'I'm looking for Tunde?'

'I'm his wife Tonia, Tunde's out working.'

'I just want to ask him some questions about his work.'

'You're welcome to come in and wait but I must warn you it's dangerous to ask him about his work.'

'Why would that be?' Maisi asks nervously.

'Because you won't be able to get him to shut up about it, once he and Lazarus start.'

'Lazarus?'

'Our son. He prefers Laz by the way.'

Tonia makes Maisi some tea and then goes back to her cooking.

At 6.30 the two appear in hi-vis gear, smelling vaguely of tarmac.

After the introductions are made Maisi produces some pictures.

'Did you do these repairs or know who did?'

Laz jumps in,

'Look, Dad, these are two of our first, remember I was only fourteen. Before we even started adding quartz.'

Tunde picks up the pictures.

'Yep, fairly crude, but you've got to start somewhere.'

'You mean there's more? How many of these *poems* have you done?'

Tunde points out a map of Shropshire on a corkboard on the kitchen wall covered with little red pins. There must be at least forty.

Maisi goes over,

'Wow, can I take a picture?'

'Sure.'

Maisi snaps the map,

'Can you help me? I had a debate with Jesus about these.'

'Jesus? He's answering these days?'

'Oh, not that Jesus, Jesus my sub-editor, he's Mexican.'

'In that case it's Hesus surely. What's the debate?'

'Well, I thought this one was *yo yo yo* whereas he liked *why oh why oh why?* Which is correct, or something else?'

'There is no right or wrong, what it means to you or whoever sees it is right.'

'Fair enough. What did you mean about quartz?'

Laz explains,

'Those early ones are just plain tarmac, then we started adding quartz for a bit of sparkle and then loads of other stuff, blue chip, red granite, feldspar. Tried everything, you name it.'

Tunde opens a box file and pulls out a list which he gives to Maisi. It details forty-three sections of roads with dates of the work. Maisi glances over it,

'Do you have pictures of these works?'

Tunde points at a series of half a dozen box files,

'Everything in here.'

'Can I see.'

'Nope, these works are designed to be seen in motion, they are kinetic, photographs just don't do it, especially the more recent pieces.'

Maisi nods,

'Fair enough, I am going to be busy. When I write this story do you want to be anonymous or can I give your names?'

'Sure you can give our names?'

'You won't get in trouble over all this.'

'Why? We do a good job, everything is within tolerances, any additional materials we pay for.'

'But don't you break up the road more than you need to?'

'Nope, first thing we do is survey the road and see what work is needed. Then we work the material into the road and vice versa.'

'Like Michelangelo freeing the figure from the block of marble.'

'Exactly, the poem is already there in the road we simply release it.'

For five weeks Maisi goes on a whirlwind tour of Shropshire's B roads. Whenever they are free she takes Carlos or Jesus to help with photos. Many times she finds herself in tears over the beauty of the work. Meanwhile, stories of Hearsay bin strikes, dog festivals, children's parades etc. all go unreported.

Five weeks later Maisi's big story hits the *Hearsay Star and Gazette*, it takes over nearly a whole *Friday Special* edition with pictures and interviews. Then the floodgates open. All the big newspapers, BBC, Sky News, and even quite a few foreign papers and TV pile in.

At first, everything is positive and then comes the backlash, starting with letters from disgruntled road users about waste, frivolity, and endangering drivers. Questions are asked about budgets, and supervision, and eventually calls for Tunde and Laz to be sacked or even prosecuted and for all the work to be destroyed. But at the same time, hordes of interested onlookers are flooding to Shropshire.

Finally, to stem the chaos Shropshire council arranges a special hearing to decide the future of the '*interpolations*' as they are now termed. Tunde and Laz don't want to attend so Maisi as their principal go-between stands in.

At the hearing, the black hats on the side of destruction of the work are principally Roads and Safety, and Shropshire Police Force. The white hats on the side for preservation are the Shropshire Tourist Board, the Arts Council, English Heritage, the Poetry Society etc..

The black hats kick off with their trump card, road safety. The deputy chief constable armed with impressive charts tells of increased road use, on minor B roads he stresses, a possible future increase in accidents, distracted drivers, not to mention inconvenience to regular road users.

The white hats however have a knight in shining armour, Prof Shaun Rubins OBE FREng Emeritus Professor of Transportation Engineering, no less, who demolishes the previous presentation with his rather clipped Mr Micawberish but decidedly authoritative speech.

'Principal cause of road accidents - driver inattention. Roadwork poems - increased attention - fewer accidents. Secondary cause of road accidents - excessive speed.' Here quite a few in the audience turn their attention to Inspector Fine who merely shrugs. 'Roadwork poetry observation - moderate speed - fewer accidents. In short, roadwork poets, I salute you, welcome safety, welcome speed limits, welcome joy on our roads.'

He gets a deserved round of applause, however, in the end the case is resolved, as so often, by the subject of money. The council treasury estimates the cost of resurfacing the forty-three sites to be around eight million whereas on the other hand increased tourism to Shropshire over the next five years from the *interpolations* could be over three hundred million of which a sizeable chunk will come the way of the council. The chairman announces,

'I don't think we need to hear any more. Case closed.' A series of resolutions are passed allowing Tunde and Laz a considerable budget for upkeep of sites and new work, an application to UNESCO for World Heritage Status should be speedily processed, special council website for promotion, council-sponsored tours and an early lunch. Happy days.

Maisi arrives at the Nweke household to tell them the good news. In addition she has just heard coincidentally that morning that one of the major publishers is interested in producing a glossy coffee table book with extensive photos and even an eBook version with the hint that she might be asked to ghost-write it.

'Just think,' she says, 'once published your work will live on, it will be immortal.'

Tunde shakes his head sadly,

'Books, you think they last? Flimsy little things, gone in a few hundred years, no, if you want work to last you need stone and gravel.'

Maisi gets the point and temporarily shelves the book idea,

'You know I have been getting lots of inquiries about your methods, others want to try it out, maybe you have started something big.'

Tunde raises his eyebrows,

'Started? You think we are the first? You're crazy. There's Lake Moeris in Egypt, the Appian Way in Italy, Siskiyou Trail in California, Nakasendo...'

'Don't forget my favourites the Tea Horse Road and the Qin Highway in China,' Laz butts in.

Maisi asks,

'You mean those roads are all...?'

Tunde nods,

'If you know how to read them, of course.'

The Tork Battles

If you drive west from the pretty market town of Hearsay on the B4699 you will encounter the lovely Tork Villages. First, after about five minutes you will enter the village of Big Tork and if you are ignoring the speed signs as most people seem to, you will be in and out in no time and a few minutes later will see the signs for Big Tork's nemesis Small Tork. If you are particularly observant you may notice that it seems to be taking slightly longer to drive through Small Tork than it took to get through Big Tork. If your interest is sufficiently piqued you may stop off at the Cafe Tocqueville (named after the famous French writer Alexis de Tocqueville who stayed there one night in 1835 intrigued no doubt by the similarity of the name of the place to his own name) in Small Tork for a coffee and a muffin and if you are lucky and get chatting to its owner Seamus you may hear the story of the Tork Battles of ninety-seven. In case you go a different route or have more pressing matters to attend here is the story exactly as he told it to me.

Ninety-seven is a hot summer and the chairman of the parish council of Small Tork, Karl, has been having a little hanky panky with Nina the local postmistress. You probably remember that when Karl's wife Emma found out about their *Close Encounter* there was a kind of *High Noon* moment outside the post office between her and Nina, but that is another story for another day.

Anyway, with quite a bit of gossip going around and as there are elections coming up in the autumn, Karl reckons he needs a little diversion from this delicate matter and decides to blow on the embers of the long-running dispute between the two Tork villages. The basis for the disagreement is the fact (already noted) that Small Tork (population 274 and a half) is in fact larger than Big Tork (population 165 and a half) despite their names suggesting otherwise.

To fan the flames Karl decides to set up a grand public debate with his counterpart, Nicko (Big Tork's parish council Registrar and default chairman) to resolve the matter. Nicko, by the way, has no indiscretions to bury and has indeed just won his elections so is safe for three years but he does like a bit of a party and also any opportunity to humiliate Karl so he readily agrees. The gloves are off, let battle commence!

As the weather is hot they have decided on an outside location and long tables are set up on the green in the neighbouring village of Happen; neutral territory to ensure fairness and an even turnout. Thanks to some excellent posters designed by the *Hearsay Star and Chronicle* sub-editor Jesus featuring Karl and Nicko - back-to-back - headshots - blowing on smoking pistols (better than it sounds, you had to see it really), quite a crowd from all three villages gathers.

The two chairmen are set up on opposite sides with their teams and you can see immediately it will be a battle of styles, Karl, despite the heat is wearing a suit and tie while Nicko has on a ripped tee shirt with a faded Metallica logo on it and is carrying a bottle of Carlsberg which he flashily opens on the table edge – he used to use his teeth but broke a molar and it cost him £700 for a new gold crown.

Marny on seeing the pair of councillors squaring up remarks that it reminds him of Muhammad Ali versus George Foreman, the *Rumble in the Jungle* (although Happen Green is rather better manicured than the Zaire bush).

Karl kicks off the debate with a lecture on the current populations, he has a whiteboard with some intricate graphs showing the recent increase in the population of Small Tork, there is some sniggering as whispering in the crowds suggests he might be responsible for some of that increase. The arrows however don't lie and there can be no doubt that the disparity between the two villages is increasing as we speak.

Over to Nicko. He stands up, takes a swig of his Carlsberg, and tells the crowd,

'Size isn't everything,' to large cheers from his supporters.

He carries on,

'Plus, we are not called Big Tork because of the size of our population, rather we are Big Tork because of the size of our hearts.' Is there a tear in his eye, surely not? Clapping now, some even from Small Torkians.

The debate is now opened up to the spectators for questions and suggestions.

Old Mina is first to stand up,

'If we split off the north of Small Tork to create a third village then what remains of Small Tork would be smaller than Big Tork. Problem solved.'

There is a general murmuring in the crowd.

Karl stands up not looking best pleased,

'Who do you think you are Mina, Goldilocks? What do you want to call this new village anyway - Baby Tork?'

Nicko for once seems to be in agreement with Karl on this one, pointing out that with the rising numbers this new village (let's say for the sake of argument it might be called Tiny Tork) could soon expand to become larger than its two counterparts and in ten years this debate could be repeated but ten times worse with some kind of Mexican three-way standoff. Mina sits down grumbling.

Fergus is next up, he runs the pharmacy in Happen and suggests the problem would be easily solved if the good people of Big Tork could be persuaded to procreate more and the people of Small Tork might abstain, or at least be careful. Someone in the crowd points out that Fergus might just be saying this to increase his sales of contraceptives on the one hand and pregnancy tests on the other?

Karl points out it would take thirty years for that scheme to make any difference anyway, much to everyone's relief, and then he goes on to propose his master suggestion,

'There is an obvious answer to this staring us all in the face - why not just switch the names of the two villages? Not only will that solve the problem but it would also save on the expense of making new road signs, we just swap them round in the middle of the night.'

Nicko is incensed,

'Big Tork will never give up its name, ever. Those precious road signs will have to be wrested from my cold dead hands!' Cheering.

Old Mina is immediately back on her feet again, she obviously had her three Weetabix that morning,

'If you are going to be so stubborn in that case why don't we just leave stupid old Big Tork as it is and change the name of Small Tork to Bigger Tork?'

General applause but Mina is on a roll,

'In fact, why not go a step further and make it Enormous Tork.'

A chant starts to build up in the crowd,

'Enormous Tork, Enormous Tork, Enormous Tork.'

Luckily at this moment, the pizza van arrives from Hearsay and the discussion is temporarily halted, after all, free pizza trumps debate any day of the week.

In the intermezzo enthusiasm for Enormous Tork abates, nobody really wants that name on their letterheads, do they?

Once everyone is pizza sated Karl asks,

'Any more suggestions?'

Maisi junior journalist raises her hand (obviously trying to stir up trouble for a good story in the *Hearsay Gazette* - at this time not yet united with the *Hearsay Star*),

'Why not merge the two into a single village, simply Tork?'

The Big Tork council secretary interjects saying this would probably lead to the merging of the two councils and thus lead to the need for only a single chairman. But which of the two would that be? Karl and Nicko look at each other nervously, it doesn't look good for especially Nicko with his smaller population. Ernest suggests that the two chairmen should strip naked and wrestle it out in the mud patch by Happen Pond, winner takes all. Marny puts his hands over his eyes and tells him,

'That horrible image will live with me for the rest of my life.'

It seems as if they are getting nowhere and the crowds are growing restless so Nicko takes the opportunity to jump on the table,

'Time for a vote, guys,' he shouts. 'A beer or coke on me for everyone who votes for the Status Quo. Who is with me, hands up.' Everyone's hand goes up except Karl. Nicko gives him a look and Karl slowly raises his hand too. Nicko passes him a beer and the real party commences to the joyful strains of *Rockin' All Over the World*.

You say Hearsay and I Say...

The pretty market town of Hearsay has no secondary school but makes up for that with its thriving Primary. At playtime, the entire town can enjoy the joyous shrieks of laughter and shouting coming from its environs.

Paulina, (daughter of the Reverend Wood and recently promoted to deputy head) was dozing her way through the morning class, the seven to eight year olds to be exact, on the third day of their first term of the year. Little Bertha puts her hand up (you may remember her from the street crossing button pushing incident, since then, she has not been backwards in coming forward, as they say).

Paulina sighs softly,

'Yes, Bertha?'

'Please, miss, is the name of our town pronounced Hearsay or Herrsay?'

Paulina sighs again. Every year, this crops up. *Why this is hell, nor am I out of it.*

At least she knows these days not to come down on either side, half the town says one and the other half the other and whichever half she supports will bring missives of retribution and damnation from the other spurned and forsaken half. On the other hand, not answering questions always looks weak and indecisive. She decides on the well-worn strategy of embarking on such a long convoluted story that by the end the class will either have forgotten the question or be so bored they won't care one way or the other. Should be a piece of cake for a professional like her,

'That is a very good question, Bertha, and to answer we must take a close look at the history of our pretty market town. Now in the Jurassic Era (she must be careful not to say Hearsay either way so decides to channel Thornton Wilder) Our Town didn't exist, which is a good thing, why, anyone?'

Billy puts his hand up and gets a nod from Paulina,

'Because it would have got stomped by the dinosaurs?'

'Well, that is indeed true, good answer, but also don't forget that at his time humans didn't yet exist so there would have been nobody to empty the bins or drive the buses or teach in the schools, so that would have been a very sorry state of affairs, wouldn't it?'

The class nods dutifully.

'Now swiftly moving forward to the Roman Era (Paulina is aware she has skipped a hundred and fifty million years, but well she hasn't got all day, has she?) there was a small settlement on this spot named Heronium Minimum and where can we see some of its old Roman walls?' She is starting to bore herself, surely a good sign in these circumstances.

Billy again,

'Down beyond the end of Moor Street, there's a plaque and everything.'

'Exactly. Moving on to the Domesday Book in 1086 we see the village of Hestre mentioned, with just thirty-three households.'

The class is satisfactorily glazing over and Paulina hasn't even got to the Tudors yet, never mind the Industrial Revolution, when out of the blue Jasper puts his hand up and says without waiting for a prompt,

'Please, miss, my uncle pronounces it Arsey.'

There is a bit of a collective gasp. Half the class look worried at this impudence, *the sheep*, half smile behind their hands, with some outright sniggering, *the goats*.

What did Jesus say to the goats? Paulina closes her eyes and thinks,

'Depart from me, you cursed, into the eternal fire which is prepared for the devil and his angels. Mathew 25/41.'

She opens her eyes but the snickering goats remain stubbornly undeparted. Jasper is even still grinning.

Paulina snaps, enough is enough.

She stands up and approaches the unfortunate boy, a bit like when *Dirty Harry* goes for the punk and asks him if he feels lucky,

'So, Jasper, your uncle is *French*, is he?'

Jasper, confused, looks around at his classmates and stutters,

'Noo.'

'But, he must be *French* if he doesn't pronounce his aitches?'

'No, he comes from Wenlock.'

Paulina ignores this denial,

'So, he's *French* and goes around singing *zere's a 'ole in my bucket, dear 'enry, dear 'enry?*'

'He doesn't have a bucket.'

'So, he eats croissants for breakfast that he dunks in a steaming bowl of café au lait.' Paulina wishes she was now sitting in some nice Parisian Café drinking a café au lait and smoking a Gauloise, or even drinking a pastis with the Tour Eiffel in the distance.

'No, he has bran flakes.'

'So, he wears a stripy shirt and rides around on a bicycle selling onions?'

'No, he's a lorry driver.'

Bertha catches on and joins in the rout,

'So, he wears a beret?'

'No, he wears a baseball cap.'

The rest of the class seeing that Bertha has got away with her intervention and also which way the tide is flowing start up a chant, softly at first,

'Beret, beret, beret.'

Gradually getting louder,

'Beret, beret, beret.'

Paulina sees that Jasper is near to tears and is overcome with a tiny particle of remorse so she holds up her hand to silence them thinking to herself,

'Beloved, do not avenge yourselves, but rather give place to wrath; for it is written, "Vengeance is Mine, I will repay," says the Lord.'

She wonders, however, just what sort of vengeance our Good Lord would want to exact for saying a bad word in class? She guesses he sort of adds the transgressions all up in a pile over your lifetime and divides them by the number of days you have suffered on the planet, then you either make the cut like those lucky golfers, or not. Well, she has saved Him the trouble today and little Jasper is a tiny step closer to heavenly bliss.

Bertha pulls Paulina out of her reverie,

'Please, Miss, you never answered my first question about the pronunciation. You were up to the Domesday book remember? So, which is it - Hearsay or Herrsay?'

The class looks at her expectantly and it seems that the best-laid plans of mice and men and primary school teachers have gone awry when Paulina hears that sweet, sweet ringing sound she loves so much.

As so often at that moment she muses to herself, *what phrase do boxers and teachers both have so much passion for?* (Of course, the two professions do share many things - trying to impose your will on another while avoiding them doing the same to you, ducking and diving, and severe bruising. On the other hand, though, I suppose teachers don't end up spitting blood into a bucket quite so often).

Oh, the phrase they both love, I nearly forgot - it is of course *Saved by the Bell.*

Welcome to
the Hotel Anorexia

For anyone visiting the pretty market town of Hearsay the number one place to rest your weary head is the Wyke Arms Hotel, run by Nenna and her brother Hector. Only four rooms and pleasantly quiet - four green dots on *Trip Advisor*, no less.

One day six months ago the Wyke Arms hosted the Bruns family from Bavaria venturing for their first time into the Shropshire wilderness. Two adults and two children, all density-challenged, if you know what I mean. On arrival, Nenna asked them what brought them to Hearsay and was told,

'Vee hav come to see the blue hills, of course.'

'Good luck with that,' Nenna tells them.

They are currently the only guests but somehow next morning at eight they manage to completely clear out the breakfast buffet single-handedly, the buffet which usually provides Nenna and Hector with their lunch from the leftovers and sometimes even a snack for tea on quiet days. Hector of course thinks the family are sneaking out some supplies for a mid-day picnic, despite the stern warning notices around the breakfast area warning not to do so.

Hector watches the Bruns family carefully next morning through the serving hatch, but no, they are not sneaking out quickly made sandwiches hidden in paper napkins but simply just eating everything in sight, they even have the temerity to ask him if there is any more ham. Hmm. After they are gone the breakfast room once again looks as if it has been laid waste by a swarm of locusts, hungry locusts at that, no free lunch for the owners today. Hector even has to make a special trip to Costco to restock their depleted larders, at some cost ironically.

That afternoon Hector on his way back from the wholesaler has a brainwave – why not charge the customers on a sliding scale according to their weight? He tells Nenna excitedly when he gets in but she immediately pooh-poohs the idea.

'You're crazy, that must be completely illegal? Isn't it fatist as well?'

Hector puts on his thinking cap over supper and comes up with a revised plan. He tells Nenna, this time in a little more circumspect fashion, he doesn't want to be shot down in flames twice in a row,

'Listen, instead of punishing the mass challenged, which I grant you does seem rather judgemental and possibly contravenes the *Equality Act 2010*, though I am not absolutely sure weight is a protected characteristic, but just to be on the safe side, what we could do instead is - reward the fit and svelte with a nice discount. Carrot rather than stick.'

Nenna however is still not convinced,

'Hector, if we give away discounts all over the place, willy nilly, we will make even less money than we are now and we are only just keeping our heads above water as it is.'

Hector is prepared for this response, however,

'What we could do is we sneak the overall price up gradually over the coming months so that when we introduce the discounts the skinnies are just paying what they do now and the biggies are paying the 'new normal' price which is more. Ta-da. We could even call it the *Sports Discount* to disguise the fact we are discriminating, those smug sporty types will be so pleased with themselves they'll be queuing up.'

Nenna is incredulous,

'*Sports Discount*? What if your sport happens to be professional darts player, or what about sumo wrestler?'

Hector blanches at this new concept, *what fresh hell is this?*

'Maybe we will get some sumo wrestler couple staying? The new Ikea bed in the bridal suite would never take it, especially if they get up to some hanky panky.'

Nenna muses on the possibility,

'Let's not worry about that, we've never ever had anyone from Japan staying in twenty years.'

Hector is not convinced,

'That doesn't prove anything. After all, we've never had anyone from Bavaria staying till recently, damn those blue hills, I wish everyone would just forget about them.'

Over the next few days Hector forgets about the sumo nightmare and gradually wears Nenna down over his new scheme. In the end, she cautiously agrees to let him set it up. Firstly, he renames the establishment as the Woke Arms (Fitness Hotel) and in the new publicity stresses the healthy salad section in the breakfast buffet and the new exercise bikes in the amenities room. Then comes the *Sports Discount* (purely voluntary to avoid any legal problems) where if you can show your BMI is under 30 you get a ten per cent discount, under 25 you get twenty per cent off (Nenna drew the line at including waist to height measurements). Next to the check-in desk Hector puts an electronic weighing machine and marks various heights on the wall for easy on-the-spot BMI verification.

At first, all goes well. Some customers refuse to consider the discount and cough up the full price, some are excited to show how fit they are and jump gladly on the scales. A few larger visitors seem a little put out.

However, Hearsay is not such a large town and as word gets around about the goings on at the Woke Hotel things start brewing.

The first Nenna knows about it is one Saturday morning when she looks out the window. There are a group of ladies in the street with some banners. They seem to be chanting tunelessly. Hector joins her at the window and asks,

'What the hell are they singing?'

Nenna opens the window a crack and puts her ear to the gap,

'It seems to be *Welcome to the Hotel Anorexia*, I think they are approximating to the tune of that old Eagles hit from the seventies.'

Now that she has said the name Hector recognises the tune and even picks up on some of the words, they seem to have adapted mostly the third verse with its catchy ending *You can check out any time you like but you can never leave.*

Later that day it starts raining and the protestors disperse.

Nenna and Hector decide to sit it out. The current guests seem confused with the demo but not unduly concerned.

Next Saturday the protest group is back and there seem to be a few more among them.

Hector asks Nenna,

'That's not the Eagles song any more, is it?'

Nenna listens once again,

'Nope, it's the Hollies now, *He's not heavy he's my brother.*'

Anyway, five weeks later Nenna and Hector decide to abandon the *Sports Discount* scheme. It's not the protestors that change their minds, in fact they were looking forward to their arrival each week and even had a little sweepstake between themselves on which new song they would choose.

No, the main deciding factor was a tongue-lashing from young journalist Maisi Dukes. At first, Hector had thought when she turned up that she was going to write a story in the *Star and Gazette* about the scheme but it turns out Maisi was on more of a personal agenda.

'What the hell do you two think you are doing?' she had told them before she was hardly in the door.

'Sorry?' answered Hector.

'Don't you know that children in the playground bully others who are different, and you are giving those bullies ammunition with your ridiculous narrow-minded scheme?'

'We didn't think,' Nenna says nervously.

'People like you seldom do, you should be ashamed of yourselves, in fact the whole of Hearsay is ashamed of you. Do you even know the meaning of the word *woke*?'

As she is leaving Hector asks anxiously,

'You're not going to put all this in your newspaper are you?'

Maisi answers curtly,

'Don't worry, I wouldn't dream of giving you the publicity.'

After she's gone Nenna tells Hector,

'She's right you know. I feel terrible.'

All Hector can come up with is,

'Oops.'

A secondary factor in the ending of the scheme was the buffet remainder; as I mentioned Nenna and Hector get their lunches from the breakfast leftovers and after five weeks Nenna had had enough (or to be exact had *not* had enough).

She had even said to Hector before the Maisi intervention,

'When you first mentioned carrot and stick six months ago, I didn't know you were talking about us dining solely on leftover raw carrot and celery sticks.'

Well, it is a truth universally acknowledged that people when on their holidays, even the smug sporty types, don't seem to want rabbit food for breakfast.

Harald Englouti

The pretty market town of Hearsay derives all its water from the Ever Reservoir some miles to the south of the town. When the reservoir was created in the thirties, they unfortunately had to flood the village of Prattel and all the occupants were forcibly evacuated, some to Hearsay itself. I guess anyone who remembers the old sunken village is now long gone and no one ever speaks of it these days.

Anyway, the Summer of 2013 was particularly dry and fine, perfect weather for cycling of course. And so one Sunday midmorning young Harald (with an A) and his friend Floss (whose real name is George Elliot but was given his nickname by some bookworm many years ago - he's never read that particular book but the name stuck and he prefers it to George) take their lives in their hands on the southern B road. Unlike their fellow DMCs as the locals refer to them (dead men cycling) they don't hug the hedgerows but cycle boldly together on the crest of the road. Any cars approaching from behind are forced to slow and hoot till the next lay by when Harald and Floss gracefully let them pass with a smile and thumbs up. Of course this kamikaze approach has its risks and if they encounter Inspector Fine at his usual Mach 0.14 they are in trouble.

Today however the roads are clear and when they spot the Ever Reservoir it seems the ideal spot for their picnic. I say picnic but it is really just a couple of cans of Heineken and a jumbo bag of crisps from Ramamurthi's.

After their feast they are lying sunning themselves on the bank when Floss notices something glinting not too far out in the lake and points it out to Harald. The two go down to the water's edge and peer out shading their eyes with their hands.

'It looks like an old man with a beard and one of those scythe things, like he's walking on the water,' says Harald.

'I think it might be a weathervane. Could be made of brass the way it's shining. There must be an old church down there holding it up.'

You can just about make out through the water the top of some stone structure under the figure. Harald and Floss get out their mobiles and start searching. Floss is fastest,

'Look, there was a village, Prattel there, look here is a pic before it was flooded. Look, there is the church with a weather vane. Exact same old guy. *Father Time* it says.'

'How deep is it, the water?' Harald asks peering over Floss's shoulder.

Floss enlarges the picture,

'Doesn't say, but looking at the height of the church I would say, twenty feet?'

Harald gets the web link from Floss and reads some more.

'Know what, Floss, I'm going to go down and visit that sunken village. Maybe there is precious stuff and valuables down there?'

'Harald, it's not like a sinking ship, the people knew about the plan to flood the place for months and had plenty of time to remove all their valuables and stuff.'

'There must be something there, it's like a kind of time capsule from eighty years ago, you know. Something not worth anything then could have been left behind and now it's an antique. Last week on eBay I saw a *Vintage 1990 Gameboy* for ninety-three thousand pounds!'

Floss pours cold water on the idea by pointing out that everything has been under *cold water* for eighty years and is either rotted or rusted away. Though probably a nineteen-thirties *Gameboy* would be pretty valuable, he concedes laughing.

Two weeks later Floss gets an excited call from Harald, who has out of the blue received a hundred and fifty quid from his gran for his eighteenth birthday and has blown nearly all of it on a *complete working shallow water diving outfit (sight unseen) free delivery.* Some guy from Walsall is bringing it in his truck. Floss nips round to Harald's next morning to find him in his backyard surrounded by boxes.

'What the ...' is all Floss can get out.

'I thought it would be just like an aqualung and a mask,' wails Harald.

Floss looks into one of the boxes, miles of tubing. Another has some weird pump thing. Harald opens a third and pulls out a brass helmet. It has writing on the side that looks like Russian. It also has a kind of handle on top and Floss lifts it up and puts it over Harald's head.

'You look like you just walked out of a *Tintin* cartoon,' he laughs.

The last two boxes contain a pair of lead boots and a canvassy suit.

Floss nods,

'Well, you certainly got your money's worth.'

They connect the pump and the miles of tube to the helmet. Harald gets a basin of water and they submerge it and Floss starts pumping, bubbles flow from under the bottom of the helmet.

'Well, I guess that's all there is to it.'

Floss agrees,

'Seems simple. Any problems with the air supply like the pipe gets snagged or I have a heart attack pumping, you just kick off your boots and head to the surface.'

The weather service is predicting welcome (for the rest of Hearsay) rain at the end of the week so there is no time to lose if the reservoir is going to start filling up again. Floss borrows his dad's pickup and they head out for the lake the next day.

You can still see the old road that leads down to the village and disappears into the water near where the two had been sitting that first day. Harald decides that will be the safest route down for him to take. By the water's edge Harald puts on the canvas suit and the lead boots and Floss lowers the helmet over his head. He attaches the air hose to the helmet; it is on a sort of spring-loaded reel.

'Not exactly rocket science,' says Floss but truth be told Harald does look like something out of a sci-fi movie or maybe even a horror film.

Floss starts pumping and with a forlorn wave, Harald marches into the water holding the tube for safety in one hand and a waterproof flashlight in the other. After his head submerges you can still see the bubbles coming up and Floss, as he is pumping, tracks Harald's progress as he gradually approaches the village.

Under the water Harald can see better than he thought. The roadway is still fairly clear and he has no problem walking down the hill. The water is cold even though it is summer and the suit gives no protection but the lead boots clump satisfyingly into the mud making him feel invincible.

Eventually he approaches the village and can just make out the church door which has all rotted away leaving only a stone arch. He has just enough pipe to get there and he carefully enters the church.

Sun rays are struggling through the higher windows into the greenish water and the whole scene looks like a painting. All the pews are rotted away too but there are some stone benches round some of the pillars. Harald sits down on one of the seats, he suddenly feels very calm. The noise of the bubbles seems less and he can hardly hear them, maybe Floss is getting tired, the poor boy is going to feel his arms tomorrow morning.

Harald tries to remember the last time he was in church. Normally he can't stand them but here he feels almost spiritual. Strangely he can somehow hear the sound of an organ, maybe even some bells and is that chanting? He stops breathing for a minute to listen better.

Frying Tonight

The pretty market town of Hearsay is the homeplace of Shropshire's finest fish restaurant *Plaice to Be* as you all know. Unfortunately, business has been waning, especially since Amanda who styles herself as the *Only Vegan in the Village* (although we should stress that with a population of over 2,743 Hearsay is most certainly a town and not a village) has been campaigning outside with a placard which says *Free Heart Attack With Every Portion* on one side and on the other, *This is a Super Place, Super-Saturated*. For a number of years she had been enjoying a serving of chips once a week but suddenly discovered they were fried in beef fat - oops.

Anyway, the owner of the establishment, one Steve Merry, decided a new name would buck up trade and that the old *Plaice to Be* was getting a bit tired - also he is completely fed up with every tenth customer saying *I saw a fish shop in Kilmarnock or York or wherever with exactly the same name - did you copy it?* He wonders just how many *Plaice to Bes* there are in the world? So, after a night up with his wife Angie and a bottle of Johnny Walker the three of them (after dismissing *Goodbye Mr Chips* - too negative, and *Thou Shalt Have a Fishy* - too long) came up with the catchy new name for the establishment - *Stephen Frys*. Steve hired *Winston's Writing on the Wall* to do some new signage and three weeks later the big green sign was up over the shop with blue dolphins stencilled on either side. New business cards were made (in the shape of little fishies) and flyers printed. Business booms and there is even a little article in the *Hearsay Star and Gazette* with some nice pictures and a special offer on a *fish supper deluxe*. Happy days.

Six weeks later, Steve gets an official-looking letter from the law firm *Eversham and Eversham*. That evening, he nervously opens it and reads it out to his wife and Johnny, who seems to be becoming a member of the family these days, especially in times of stress.

Dear Mr Merry,

It has come to our notice that you have recently renamed your establishment 'Stephen Frys'. As we are the representatives of the celebrated author and TV star and feel that this name change could be confusing to his many and various fans, we insist that you change the name to an alternative forthwith. Failure to do so within the next three weeks will leave us no alternative but to seek substantial damages. Blah blah.

Angie looks a little worried,

'Don't forget Steve, you already have a criminal record.'

'That was only a caution,' he answers. (In case you are wondering one evening two years ago a big Mercedes was parked outside their place and its alarm started. After three hours Steve couldn't take it any longer so he went out with a Stanley knife and was walking around the car putting some hefty scratches on it to remind the owner to set the alarm cut-off when up drove a police car. Hmm. So, a six-hundred-pound damages fine and an official caution was his reward.)

Anyway, getting back to the letter, Steve is of course reluctant to reverse his upturn in business (plus the new sign cost him £435 plus VAT) so he writes back to the lawyers letting them know that he is himself called Stephen and that he does actually fry in the shop. What is more, the name omits the tell-tale apostrophe which might lead to misinterpretation and confusion over ownership of the establishment.

The good lawyers are obviously well educated (as judged by their exorbitant fees) and swiftly write back that the third person singular present indicative of fry is fries and not frys. They suggest he renames his shop Stephen Fries, which they would be perfectly happy with. If not, they will reluctantly have to pursue the matter, as they hinted at before, through the courts, in which case they hope he has deep pockets.

Unfortunately, Steve's pockets are decidedly shallow, especially at the moment, but anyone who knows him knows that he is not one to back off in the face of adversity, sixteen years of staring into an abyss of chip fat have given him a certain stoical resilience, not to mention the monthly scrub out of the frying vats (unfortunately at room temperature beef dripping is all too solid unlike the less tasty vegetable oil that vegan Amanda is gunning for). After hours of online searching, he decides the simplest solution is to change his name by *Deed Poll* to Stephen Fry.

The cost is £42.44, which is cheaper than a new sign at any rate. He asks the authorities if he can get half price as his first name is already Stephen and so he is only changing fifty per cent of his name? A polite woman from the Royal Courts of Justice explains patiently that it is a fixed fee and helpfully tells him that one Juan Martinez Garcia Lopez Garcia de Santos paid exactly the same to change his name to Juan Garcia (only one Garcia now) who was sick of not being able to get his name into the EasyJet surname box, as did Michael Smellie who only changed a single letter (e to i that is) for other rather obvious reasons.

Stephen coughs up the full fee and writes a nice letter to the lawyers with his new name and signature (that he spent several hours perfecting).

Unfortunately, Steve only consulted with Johnny W about the Deed Poll and not his wife who is put out to now be a Mrs Merry who is married to a Mr Fry. What if they were to sign in to some hotel with different names, a little hanky panky might be inferred? Steve's less than helpful suggestion that she also changes her name to Mrs Fry (he will cough up the forty-two quid fee even) is met with disdain.

Even worse news comes, a letter from the distinguished lawyers now informs him that since their last communication they have gone and trademarked their client's name which now appears in their correspondence accompanied by a little ®. It looks like the end of the line for Steve's endeavour and he is already regretting not having kept the old *Plaice to Be* signage when out of the blue...

Shropshire's leading comedy actor (you all know who I am talking about) is one of Steve's best customers and is one evening in the green room of the Graham Norton show when in walks one of the other guests, yes, you guessed, the great man himself. Our friend tells Mr Fry the whole story, of which he was totally unaware, and which leaves him heartily amused.

Mr Fry immediately stands down his trusty attack lawyers and writes to our Steve informing him that he has his blessing and that next time he is in the vicinity he will partake of his finest fish supper with relish. Sure enough he is as good as his word and five weeks later appears to the delight of all and sundry in the town.

The front-page picture of the *Hearsay Star and Gazette* has the two gentlemen shaking hands outside the restaurant with the bold caption - *Stephen Fry meet Stephen Fry!*

Fructus Sucosus

The pretty market town of Hearsay actually has three licensed premises but the one we are going to pop into tonight is rather special; it used to be called The Armed Man, but Henry, the owner, changed it two years ago to The Office (seems to be a lot of business name changing in Hearsay these days, must be something in the air). He was hoping to drum up some more business as his customers could now tell their wives they were stuck at the office or some such nonsense. That masterplan (which he stole from somewhere anyway) never worked and the only casualty was Bernard Haitink who actually does work late at his office and seldom drinks and who does often phone his wife late to say he is stuck at the office, hmm.

Anyway, tonight, the only occupants of The Office as usual are Henry polishing glasses behind the bar and Elgin sitting at the counter. Elgin is about eighty, and some of the Hearsay children like to joke that he has lost his marbles, but to me, he seems to have his priorities in good order. As normal he is sitting with his one beer of the evening. The locals can tell the time by looking in and noting how full his glass is, if it is half full it must be eight o'clock, quarter full then nine-thirty, you get the idea. Tonight, the glass tells us it must be just after nine when in comes a stranger, a salesman type with a large heavy suitcase. He asks Henry where the toilet is and gets a nod of the head to the door at the back of the bar. On his return, doing himself up, he senses a slight atmosphere and realises he had better buy a drink before he leaves, so he sits down at the bar along from Elgin and asks for a beer. Elgin casually sends a subliminal, flickering glance up at the ceiling and the guy looks up to see what looks like a playing card stuck up there. He glances a question at Henry who deftly deflects the glance to Elgin who then deflects the gaze to his glass. The little ballet of glances, or is it a little football passing sequence, is clear and the new guy gets the message,

'Another beer for my good friend here who no doubt has an interesting story?'

Elgin downs his previous beer in one and waits expectantly till his new full beer is placed in front of him. Time in this universe has been reset to a new dimension and any passers-by who happen to look in now will be scratching their heads at the earliness of the hour.

Elgin takes his first sip bringing us up to only ten past six and begins his story,

'One evening nine years ago there was a terrible storm.'

Henry stops polishing and listens carefully, he has heard the story a hundred times before but Elgin always adds in a few new details every telling and he doesn't want to miss out.

'Suddenly, the door flies open and in rushes this guy, soaking wet. Henry, here, gives him a bar towel to dry his face and I shut the door against the elements, nobody else in the bar that night. Apparently, this guy's car has broken down just outside the town and his mobile was out of battery. He asked to use the bar phone to call a garage and a taxi.'

Elgin runs his finger round the top of his glass – if it was a wineglass, it would sing a clear note but it just vibrates dully.

'You have many taxis round here?' the sales guy asks casually.

Elgin shakes his head.

'Not at that time of night, Max sometimes pretends to be a taxi but by then he would be rather far gone. No choice but to order one from Flax, that takes at least forty minutes, so the guy has a pint and some crisps while he is waiting. Anyway, you'll never guess who it was?'

'Who?'

'Only Frank Beecher, you know, the magician.'

'Yeh?' the guy nods tentatively, 'rings a bell?'

'You must remember Frank, he came second in Britain's Got Talent, he lost to that little girl with the pigtails that whistled the Queen of the Night from the Magic Flute?'

'Oh yeah? I remember her. Didn't she close one nostril with her finger at a certain point to make a kind of humming harmony with the whistling? Brought the house down?'

'Exactly. She had it in the bag of course, but our boy gave her a good run for her money, any other year the title would have been his. Anyway, this Frank Beecher gets himself a second beer and asks if me and Henry want to see a trick? Of course, we says yes. So he takes out a pack of cards and asks me to pick one. I get the seven of clubs. He asks me to sign it without showing it to him and then put it back in the pack. I does as he says keeping a close eye in case I see any funny business but it all looks above board. Then, just as he is shuffling the pack he goes and slips off his stool and the cards go flying everywhere. Well of course me and Henry here help pick them all up and dust him down but of course the trick is ruined. He still asks me to find my card anyway, I look through the pack, it's not in there, and then,' dramatic pause from Elgin, 'he looks up at the ceiling and way up there is my card with my signature on it. Been there to this day.'

The sales guy kneels up on his stool to get a closer look at the card apparently stuck to the roof. Henry looks a bit anxious about health and safety, last time someone slipped on a beer puddle his insurance went up by a third.

The sales guy pops his glasses on to read the signature,

'Elgin?'

'That's me. That card has been there like I said, nine years.'

The guy jumps back down and rubs his chin thoughtfully,

'Chewing gum, it's got to be, you know I work for Spar's small items so I should know, sticks like anything.'

Elgin scratches his head,

'Come to think of it, now you mention it, he was chewing when he came in and not when he left.'

Henry nods in agreement.

'*Ecce provatum est,*' the business guy pronounces.

'Come again?'

'Latin, it means, *see it is proven.*'

Elgin asks,

'You speak Latin?'

'Yep, have to, I do all the Vatican Spar small item deliveries, they love chewing gum down there in Roma, all that endless talking in those little boxes - *masticando gummi* they call it. You should see the marble floor outside the Sistine after one of them conclaves, absolutely disgusting, drives the cleaners mad.' The business guy then leans in and whispers, 'just between us three I'm working on a new gum recipe, one that doesn't stick.'

Elgin nods,

'But isn't the stickiness what makes it chewy? If you take that away?'

'My secret is that the new gum is still sticky but only when moist. Once it dries out it just falls off anything it's stuck to, sweep it up with a plain old brush, could make my fortune and I get out of all this trekking around, but not a word to anyone.'

Elgin nods and zips his lips closed before taking a sip of beer,

'Interesting. Getting back to Roma, what about the Pontiff, is he a chewer?'

'Oh yeh, one of the worst, he likes the old *fructus sucosus.*'

'*Fructus sucosus?*'

'*Juicy Fruit.*'

'Like in that *Cuckoo's Nest* film?' Henry joins in for the first time.

'Exactly. Don't remind me about *Cuckoo's Nest.* The year that film came out was a golden year for the gum trade. It simply flew off the shelves. And what's more, they didn't pay a penny for it. Product placement like that nowadays you're talking two hundred thousand minimum. Happy days.'

The sales guy looks at his watch, finishes his beer and picks up his suitcase,

'No rest for the wicked.'

He takes one last look at the ceiling.

'Chewing gum, definitely, spearmint regular at a guess, that's the stickiest,' he comments on his way out.

Elgin nods for the umpteenth time this evening and then busies himself getting to work on bringing time in The Office back in line with that in the outside world.